THIS BOOK BELONGS TO

. . . .

I CELEBRATED WORLD BOOK DAY 2020 WITH THIS BRILLIANT GIFT FROM MY LOCAL BOOKSELLER AND SIMON & SCHUSTER
#SHAREASTORY

BOOKS ARE RUBBISH!

Sue Hendra & Paul Linnet

CELEBRATE STORIES. LOVE READING.

This book has been specially created and published to celebrate World Book Day. **World Book Day** is a charity funded by publishers and booksellers in the UK and Ireland. Our mission is to offer every child and young person the opportunity to read and love books by giving you the chance to have a book of your own. To find out more, and for loads of fun activities and reading recommendations to help you to keep reading, visit **worldbookday.com**

World Book Day in the UK and Ireland is also made possible by generous sponsorship from **National Book Tokens** and support from authors and illustrators.

World Book Day works in partnership with a number of charities, who are all working to encourage a love of reading for pleasure.

BookTrust is the UK's largest children's reading charity. Each year they reach 3.4 million children across the UK with books, resources and support to help develop a love of reading. **booktrust.org.uk**

The National Literacy Trust is an independent charity that encourages children and young people to enjoy reading. Just 10 minutes of reading every day can make a big difference to how well you do at school and to how successful you could be in life. **literacytrust.org.uk**

The Reading Agency inspires people of all ages and backgrounds to read for pleasure and empowerment. They run the Summer Reading Challenge in partnership with libraries; they also support reading groups in schools and libraries all year round. Find out more and join your local library. **summerreadingchallenge.org.uk**

World Book Day also facilitates fundraising for:

Book Aid International, an international book donation and library development charity. Every year, they provide one million books to libraries and schools in communities where children would otherwise have little or no opportunity to read. **bookaid.org**

Read for Good, who motivate children in schools to read for fun through its sponsored read, which thousands of schools run on World Book Day and throughout the year. The money raised provides new books and resident storytellers in all the children's hospitals in the UK. **readforgood.org**

It was night-time in the supermarket and the veggies had been happily reading for hours.

Then crash, bang, in stomped The Evil Pea.
"Why are you all so quiet?
What are you up to?"

"We're reading!" said the veggies.

"My book is called
Exciting Electronics
– it shows you how
things work,"
said Carrot.

"Mine is a story
about a unicorn,"
said Cucumber.

"My book," said Tomato,
"is called Knitting
for Beginners."

"Knitting for Nitwits, more like!" snorted the pea.
"What a waste of time. Books are rubbish
– everyone knows that!

There's only one thing books **are** good for…"
And with that he started to pile them up,
higher and higher…

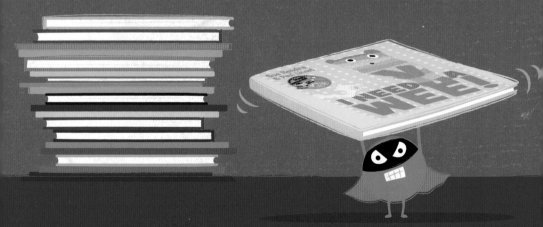

all the way
to the ceiling.
"Let's see them...

try and
read...

FUSE **OFF**

BOX **ON**

Click!

... in the DARK!"

Luckily, Aubergine found a torch
but when she shone it upwards,
everyone gasped!

"OH NO!"
panicked
the pineapples.

"HELP!"
cried the veggies,
bumping into each other in the dark.

Ouch!

Aubergine shone her torch,
"Tomato, how can you knit
at a time like this?!"

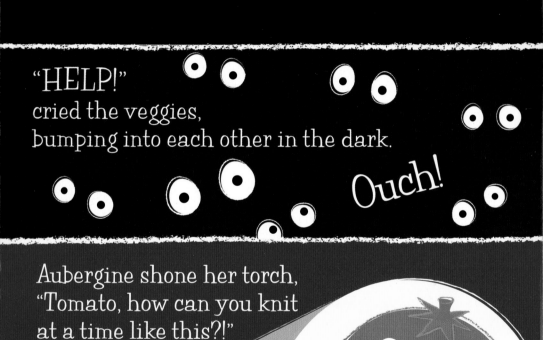

It was chaos!
And Supertato was nowhere to be seen.

What would save them this time?

Carrot used her electronic super skills... to fix the light!

Bing!

USE OFF
BOX ON

Tomato used his knitting know-how... to knit a net!

Boing!

And Cucumber used magical, mystical, rainbow twinkle-tastic sparkles... to make the world a better place!

With danger averted and the lights back on, the veggies decided it was time to deal with the pea.

"You've gone a step too far this time," said the veggies.

"There's no such thing as a step too far!"
shouted the pea.

But as it turned out, the pea was wrong.

"Sorry to hear you've hurt yourself,
Pea," said Supertato, "but don't you worry,
we know just what you're going to need
while you're getting better...

some good
books to read!"

Grrr